Snow White and the Seven Dwarfs

by Fran Hunia
illustrated by Brian Price Thomas

Ladybird Books Loughborough

This is Snow White.

She is a good girl,

and she is beautiful.

**All children have
a great ambition to read
to themselves . . .**

*and a sense of achievement when they can do so.
The* **read it yourself** *series has been devised to
satisfy their ambition. Since many children learn
from the Ladybird Key Words Reading Scheme,
these stories have been based to a large extent
on the Key Words List, and the tales chosen are
those with which children are likely to be familiar.*

*The series can of course be used as
supplementary reading for any reading scheme.
Snow White and the Seven Dwarfs is intended
for children reading up to Book 4c of the Ladybird
Reading Scheme. The following words are
additional to the vocabulary used at that level –*

Snow, White, beautiful, lives, queen,
magic, mirror, wall, who, fairest, of,
day, angry, forest, kill, dwarfs, dead,
poison, black, cloak, bite, falls,
prince, picks, piece, poisoned, marry,
as, if, think, so, seven *(in title only)*

*A list of other titles at the same level will be
found on the back cover.*

Snow White lives

with a beautiful queen.

The queen has

a magic mirror.

The queen likes to look

in her magic mirror.

She says,

"Mirror, mirror, on the wall,

Who is the fairest of us all?"

The mirror says,

"You are the fairest,"

and the queen is pleased.

One day the queen

looks into her magic mirror

and says,

"Mirror, mirror, on the wall,

Who is the fairest of us all?"

The mirror says,

"Snow White is the fairest."

The queen is angry.

She says to a man,

"Go with Snow White
and kill her."

Snow White and the man

go off into the forest.

Snow White says,

"Please do not kill me.

I will make my home

here in the forest.

You can say

that you killed me.

I will not go home

to the queen."

"Off you go then,"

says the man.

Snow White goes off

into the forest.

She sees a little white house.

She stops to look at it.

Snow White looks
into the little house.

No one is at home.

She goes in.

All the things in the house
are little.

Snow White gets into one
of the little beds.

21

Some dwarfs live in the little house.

They come home and see
Snow White in bed.

"Who is this girl?"
they say.

Snow White gets up.

She sees the dwarfs.

"Please help me," she says.

"The queen wants to kill me."

"You can live here with us,"

say the dwarfs.

Snow White thanks the dwarfs.

The dwarfs go off

into the forest to work,

and Snow White works

in the house all day.

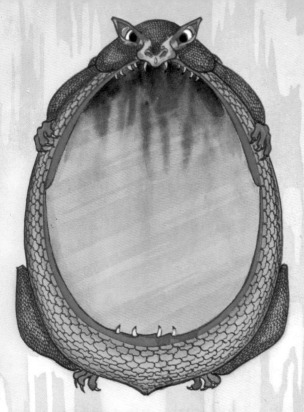

One day the queen

looks into her magic mirror

and says,

"Mirror, mirror, on the wall,

Who is the fairest of us all?"

The mirror says,

"Snow White is the fairest."

"What?" says the queen.

"Snow White is not here.

She is dead."

"No," says the mirror.

"Snow White is not dead.

She lives with some dwarfs

in a little white house

in the forest."

The queen is angry.

"I have to kill Snow White,"

she says.

She gets some apples.

One of the apples

is big and red.

The queen puts poison

on the big red apple.

The queen puts on her black cloak.

She goes to look for Snow White.

She comes

to the little white house

and says, "Can I come in?"

Snow White looks to see
who is there.

The queen says,
"Here is a big red apple
for you."

She gives Snow White

the apple with poison on it.

Snow White likes apples.

She thanks the queen
and has one bite
of the apple.

Then she falls down

as if she is dead.

The queen is pleased.

The queen goes home

and looks in her magic mirror.

She says,

"Mirror, mirror, on the wall,

Who is the fairest of us all?"

"You are the fairest,"

says the mirror.

The dwarfs come home
and think that Snow White
is dead.

"What can we do?"
they say.

A prince comes to the house.

He sees Snow White
and stops to look at her.

"What a beautiful girl," he says.

He picks Snow White up,
and the piece of poisoned apple
falls from her mouth.

Snow White looks
at the prince.

The prince says to Snow White,

"Please marry me."

"Yes," says Snow White.

She thanks the dwarfs,
and then she goes away
with the prince.

The queen says to her mirror,
"Mirror, mirror, on the wall,
Who is the fairest of us all?"

"Snow White is the fairest,
and she is going to marry
the prince," says the mirror.

The queen is so angry

that she falls down dead.

50

Snow White and the prince

get married.

Everyone is very happy.